Evert A. Duyckinck

Memorial of John Allan

Evert A. Duyckinck

Memorial of John Allan

ISBN/EAN: 9783337092740

Printed in Europe, USA, Canada, Australia, Japan

Cover: Foto ©Raphael Reischuk / pixelio.de

More available books at **www.hansebooks.com**

MEMORIAL

OF

JOHN ALLAN.

MEMORIAL

OF

JOHN ALLAN.

PRINTED FOR THE BRADFORD CLUB.
NEW YORK:
1864.

TWO HUNDRED AND FIFTY COPIES PRINTED.

We love the page that draws its flavour
From draftsman, etcher and engraver.

The Rev. James Beresford's " Bibliosophia."

Thus our time may we pass with rare books and rare friends,
Growing wiser and better till life itself ends:
And may those who delight not in black letter lore,
By some obsolete act be sent far from our shore.

"Rational Madness." A Song for the Lovers
of Curious and Rare Books, to the tune of
Liberty Hall, in Mr. Allan's Collection.

MEMORIAL.

The following memorial has been prepared in compliance with the wishes of a few friends of the late Mr. Allan, members of the BRADFORD CLUB, who desire to preserve some record of his amiable personal qualities and of the refined pursuits by which he was distinguished. There is nothing, indeed, in the account of his life, to challenge a place among the important biographies of these stirring times; and no effort will here be made to place the subject of this sketch, by any exaggeration, in a position abhorrent to his unobtrusive character. The whole story is simply this. He was a kind hearted man, fond of literature and art; plain in his habits, manly in his opinions: he enjoyed a well deserved reputation for probity and honor, and at his death left a valuable collection of rare books, engravings and other curiosities, which he had gathered about him, the amusement and solace of a long life and an unfailing resource to his companions, and which, as they are now dispersed and have become the ornaments of many private libraries, bear witness to the tastes of

2

their late owner, and, in a posthumous way, widen the circle of his acquaintance.

John Allan was born in the parish of Kilburnie, Ayreshire, Scotland, on the 26th of February, 1777. His father was a tenant farmer of the district, and the family had occupied the acres from which he gained his subsistence for more than a century. They preserved the industry and virtues which have ever marked the better classes of the Scottish cultivators of the soil; among which, we may be sure, a proper attention to intellectual discipline was not neglected. John Allan reaped the benefit of these home influences in the promotion of a manly character, while he received a sound elementary education, including instruction in Latin at a neighboring grammar school. He was always in pursuit of knowledge, and the incident is remembered in his family of his devoting the small savings from his pocket allowance, his "sugar money," in his childhood, to subscription to a newspaper.

Being the eldest of the family, he was naturally looked to for assistance in the work on the farm; but for this species of toil, and, indeed, for hard labor of any kind, he seems to have had no great inclination. When any unusual effort was required he was often out of the way; his tastes ran in a different direction: a book was in his boyhood more welcome to him than the plough, and he was already looking forward to a career in which he might gain his livelihood in some less exacting vocation. At the age of seventeen he

formed his resolution to emigrate to America, and try
his fortune in the New World. After some opposition
the family finding his determination fixed fell in with
his plans, made a purse for his benefit, and he departed
with their blessing. On his arrival at New York there
was some expectation that he would purchase land in
the interior and settle upon it; but once released from
the thraldom of the paternal farm, he had no disposition to return to the vocation. He speedily found
occupation in the city as a clerk, or bookkeeper, and
soon acquired such a reputation for industry and integ-
rity, that he was never henceforth without lucrative
employments of this kind. He was for many years
bookkeeper to Messrs. Rich and Disbrow, merchant
tailors of the city, who were largely engaged in business, and became so established in their confidence
that he was left, by each member of the firm, executor
of his will. He survived them both, and long discharged the duties thus imposed upon him, outliving
every one of the Rich family and two generations of
the Disbrows. To his clerkships, Mr. Allan at one
time added the business of a commission agent, re-
ceiving various consignments from his friends in Scotland, among whom was Mr. John M. Duncan, a Glas-
gow publisher and author of two volumes of Travels
in the United States, who sent him his books for sale.
Later in life, Mr. Allan was much employed as a house
agent or collector of rents. From these and kindred
sources, aided by a frugal habit of living, he secured
the means of independent living. He married early

in life, became a householder, occupying for a quarter
of a century a house in Pearl street facing Centre
street, the site of which is now part of the public street.
From Pearl street he removed about the year 1837 to
a commodious house, number 17 Vandewater street,
where he continued to reside, spite of all change in the
neighborhood, till his death. His acquaintances who
visited him in his last years, found him almost the only
one remaining of the old inhabitants of the street,
which when he first took up his abode there numbered
many influential citizens of the time, particularly
among the Quaker population of the city. The street
was then distinguished by its neatness, and, the lots
being deep, there were many pretty gardens with fruit
trees in the vicinity, so that the locality afforded, altogether, an agreeable residence. Of late, all this was
entirely changed ; the old families had been broken up
by death or removed to make way for the march of
improvement, the first fruits of which were the clearing
away of the gardens to give place to closely built fac-
tories and tenement houses, which became the home
of a squalid population. The street speedily swarmed
with petty groceries, lager beer shops and other ap-
pendages of a poor and crowded tenantry. It had
become, outwardly viewed, one of the most unpleasant
parts of the city to live in. Mr. Allan's friends sometimes expressed their wonder to him, asking why he
remained ; to which he would reply urging the force
of habit, and meeting the objection to the street with
the good humored remark, that " he lived in the house

—he did not live in the street." The house, it is hardly necessary to remark, was a model of neatness and cleanliness, within and without. Its white door and polished knocker were always true to the better days of the neighborhood; while the visitor on his entrance, was struck by the air of cheerfulness which the quaint old furniture, the rare prints on the walls, and the various objects of interest on all sides inspired.

A first view of all these things was doubtless much more impressive by contrast with the vicinity. Few of those who made the acquaintance of Mr. Allan of late years, particularly of those who appreciated his tastes, will forget their sensations on admission to his well stocked rooms, filled on all sides with curious objects of interest, the attraction of which, we may add, was much enhanced by the hospitable welcome and sprightly manners of the possessor. Many will recall the simple back parlor, the usual reception room, the time-seasoned early impressions of Wilkie's best works on the walls, the portrait of Burns, and hanging in kindly familiarity over the mantel the pictures of Thomas Dowse, of Cambridge, the genuine L. L. D., Learned Leather Dresser, and the nonagenarian Anderson the wood engraver, oldest of the companions of Mr. Allen, who has survived to execute the cut of his friend which graces the title page of his sale catalogue Flanking these on each side of the apartment, were the deeply laden book cases, holding the Dibdins, the Knickerbockers, the Bartolozzis, and others of those choicely illustrated books which have called forth

such eager competition ; while a series of drawers were
filled with the old watches and other more purely antiquarian curiosities of the virtuoso's collection.   Above
stairs, the book cases with their valuable contents were
repeated with the addition of a small museum of highly
polished minerals—in which beauteous marvels of nature the owner delighted—and the eye of the visitor
was further attracted in one of the rooms by a re-
markable assemblage quaintly arranged about the fire
place, of strange heathen war weapons, in which sharp-
ened Malay creases, Norman battle axes, Indian toma-
hawks, carved South Sea braining clubs, a heavy eagle-
hilted Roman sword, were curiously intermingled.   It
was the sleeping room of Mr. Allan ; and as we looked
upon the display, we could not but imagine the motley
exhibition disturbing the dreams of the rash collector—
a splendid equipment, indeed, for a night mare in which
the savage combats of all nations might be blended.
In the corner of the room stood the bright musket
which Mr. Allan, already become an American citizen,
had shouldered in the war of 1812 when in the days of
Governor Tompkins the respectability of New York
was summoned to work in the trenches, haply at that
time in anticipation only of a foreign enemy who never
made his appearance.   These warlike associations of
the room, however, were tempered by the presence of
the choice collection of books of Emblems and Missals,
a sacred and peaceful host appealing to the devotional
feeling of the worshipper of the antique, which graced
the secretary by the window in the sunniest spot in the

house. In this room thus quaintly garnished, doubtless many of our friend's happiest hours were passed,
and here at length the silver cord was loosened and
his spirit passed away from earth.

That event, which happeneth to all, came gradually
upon him, with but little roughness in the visit of the
dreaded Angel—as cheerfully regarded by him, perhaps, as by any. He had lived too long, and attended
too many friends to the grave, to be unacquainted with
the messenger of whose coming every object of anti-
quity around him was an eloquent preacher. We re-
member calling upon him one Sunday afternoon, and
finding him with a rare emblematic volume in his
hand, one of the numerous books which he possessed
of its class, Holbein's old workmanship, perhaps—
figuring the Dance of Death—as sober a homily, certainly, as was listened to that day in any of the city
churches. The lesson was habitually before him, and
contrary to the remark of Dr. Johnson, who, on view-
ing the treasures which one of his friends had gathered
in his house, said, "these are the things which make a
death bed terrible," he was accustomed to speak of the
future disposition of his books with equanimity, without shuddering at the thought. Others had lived and
died that he might enjoy ; he must not grudge posterity
its share of the accumulating benefit. We recall once
meeting him at Mr. Sabin's auction room previous
to the sale of the extensive library of the late Mr. Bur-
ton, the actor, and mentioning the proverb, " Where-
soever the carcase is, there will the eagles be gathered

together." The familiar saying pleased his fancy, and whenever we again met on a similar occasion, there was some allusion to "the eagles."

The cheerful old age of Mr. Allan, indeed, was one of the most noticeable things to observe in him. Of light frame, at no period what would be called robust, he was yet enabled after passing through a single dangerous illness—a severe attack of quinsy sore throat in middle life—to experience almost unintermitted good health during his long career of fourscore and upwards. A humorous anecdote is remembered of this illness, which may be worth repeating, pleasantly illustrating, as it does, the tastes of the collector. As Mr. Allan was lying speechless on his bed nearly suffocated by his malady, the female attendants in the room, on a hint from the physician, endeavored to rouse him to some strong emotion, hoping that the effort would break the perilous abscess which oppressed his breathing. The method which they took was characteristic and exhibited a knowledge of the ruling passion of the man. "Well, it's pretty well over with Mr. Allan now," said one of his family; "we may as well divide his books,"—and in full sight of the patient one began to take down one choice volume, a second, another, disputing affectedly over its appropriation, looking upon this as an effectual irritant, the owner meanwhile unable to speak, shaking his fist in defiance of what reasonably appeared to him an extraordinarily cool proceeding. Happily the lover of books on whom this severe experiment was tried, was speedily relieved of his malady, when a prompt word of explanation set at rest his seemingly well warranted suspicions of his friends.

Mr. Allan's good health was something noticeable. A junior "brother collector" at one time thinking his friend's sands were well nigh run, made interest to gain possession, at his death, of a certain volume which he coveted in his library; but Mr. Allan survived his eager acquaintance, and lived on quietly enjoying his books many years. It is rare, indeed, to find a man of his advanced life with so few of the physical infirmities of age upon him. His freedom of motion was unimpaired to the end. Within a short time of his death he might be met visiting the print shops in Broadway, on foot, two miles from his home, the usual limit of his pilgrimages, for he was a devoted New Yorker, seldom leaving the city on any occasion. A cheerful humor, with an unfailing supply of nervous energy, enabled him to throw off care, while the gentle tastes which he indulged as an amateur of the arts, with their innocent amusements, and, more than all, the society of his beloved daughter, after the death of his wife many years since, sole companion of his household, by whom every want was anticipated and every indulgence supplied, undoubtedly fed the sources of youthful feeling which seemed never to desert him. The visits of his friends always gave him pleasure. A call from the late Dr. Francis or from Mr. Gulian C. Verplanck, whose writings he cherished, was remembered by him with peculiar satisfaction. He identified them with American history and literature, for which he had acquired

3

a peculiar fondness, engrafting the study upon his na-
tive Scotticism.   Mr. John R. Bartlett, of Providence,
seldom visited New York without finding his way to
Vandewater street. With Dr. Koecker and other valued
friends, of Philadelphia, he shared with Mr. Allan a
fondness for his pursuits, in which they mutually assisted
one another.   Mr. Livermore, of Cambridge, was his
correspondent and occasional visitor.   Of New York-
ers, the brothers Moreau stood among the foremost in
his regard.   The friendship was of long standing and
cemented by many kindly offices. They were con-
stantly to be met with at Mr. Allan's fireside.   Mr.
James Lawson, his fellow countryman, an appreciator
of his pursuits, kept alive an acquaintanceship of many
years to the end.   Mr. Gowans, the publisher and
antiquarian bookseller of Nassau street, was an old and
valued intimate, for whose judgment Mr. Allan had
great respect.

In his younger days Mr. Allan had mingled freely
in the social circles of his countrymen, and had taken
an active part in their public festivities, as an interesting series of cards of admission to the annual Caledo-
nian balls, engraved with various devices planned by
himself, bears witness. The cards were frequently inscribed with mottoes, from old Scottish poets and other
sources appropriate to the designs which exhibit no
little variety of good humor.

One incident, pleasantly varying the monotony of
Mr. Allan's quiet career, should not be forgotten,—
the surprise party of his friends who, having made

their preparations by appointment, dropped in upon
him at his home the evening of his eightieth birth day,
February 26, 1857. A valuable scrap book, amply
decorated, which the receiver soon stored with specimens of his best drawings and engravings, remains in
the possession of his daughter, an interesting memorial
of the occasion. One of its opening pages, written in
Mr. Allan's careful and ornamental hand writing, the
excellence of which age had little diminished, tells the
story of its presentation,— how it was prepared at the
expense of his friends and delivered by Dr. Koecker,
"with a suitable speech," while on the same evening,
"I was presented by F. J. Dreer, Esq., of Philadelphia,
with an elegant gold stud, faced with a small portion of
the bell that first pealed the 'Declaration of Independ-
ence' on the memorable Fourth of July, 1776; and by
E. J. Woolsey, of Astoria, with a medal of myself prepared by him expressly for the occasion." At the re-
quest of Mr. Allan, the page on which this was recorded was signed by his friendly visitors, several of
whom, younger men, preceded him to the grave. The
signatures are Leonard R. Koecker, Fred. J. Dreer,
Joseph Moreau, John B. Moreau, Charles C. Moreau,
John Wiley, Benson J. Lossing, J. S. Phillips, P.
Hastie, Wm. J. Davis, Wm. Menzies, E. J. Woolsey,
Geo. P. Putnam.

Mr. Allan's fondness for his young visitors, was a
kindly trait of his character. Nothing gave him more
pleasure than to enlist them in his pursuits ; for which
there was often sufficient attraction in the interesting

nature of the things which employed his attention.
For Mr. Allan, as the reader has observed, was no mere
morose student of black letter, but a genial lover of
the arts, who delighted to assemble objects of the
beautiful around him.   Nor only so, but to an appreciator of his tastes he was a liberal dispenser of his
treasures.   Thus he would encourage one in the study
of the natural world by gifts of rare and valuable specimens of minerals, from his attractive stock ; while he
was ever ready to strip certain huge scrap books — re-
positories of out of the way prints — for the benefit of
youthful amateurs whom he had taught the simple
mysteries of inlaying — eagerly conferring upon them
portraits and landscapes, unattainable at Dexter's, and
encouraging their labors in the pleasing art of "illustration."   One of the most skillful adepts in this craft,
Mr. Charles C. Moreau, recalls this friendly service of
Mr. Allan, as he turns over the leaves of his choicely
illustrated "Halleck;" the writer of this sketch also
gratefully cherishes sundry free will offerings, effi-
gies of authors of by-gone centuries, contributions to
his "Pursuits of Literature ;" and others, glancing at
their portfolios, might doubtless render a similar ac-
knowledgment.   A son of one of Mr. Allan's most
esteemed friends, Mr. Menzies, points with pride to
the collection of minerals which he was led to form
by his visits to Vandewater street.

By such influences as these we have enumerated, life
was prolonged beyond the natural limit. They gave an
object to existence which old men, retired from active

pursuits, often need, and sometimes sink earlier for the want of. When death came, it was a gradual failing, during a few weeks confinement to his house, of the vital powers of the body which left the mind clear and vigorous to the end. He gave minute directions concerning the disposition of his affairs and the sale of his library, for the benefit of his only surviving child, Mrs. Stewart, whom he had appointed sole executrix of his estate. With an interest characteristic of a genuine collector, he particularly enjoined that a large paper catalogue of his library should be printed. Nothing would seem to have been neglected by him. His death occurred on the 19th of November, 1863, in the eighty-seventh year of his age. The funeral services were performed at St. Paul's Episcopal church, by his friend the Rev. Dr. Morgan Dix, when the remains were interred at Greenwood.

The true monument of an antiquarian is the catalogue of his collections. On its title page might be placed for a motto a parody of the famous inscription written on the tombstone of the licentiate Pedro Garcias, as narrated by Le Sage in his model preface to Gil Blas. As that famous legend recorded that the soul of Pedro was buried beneath, so we may write — *Here lies the soul of the departed virtuoso;* and as the cunning student of Salamanca was led to explore the grave, and was rewarded for his pains by finding the purse of the deceased licentiate, so one may not go much amiss, nor altogether lose his labor, by searching

among his books and curiosities for the passions of the
collector.　He will be sure to find there no little of the
man.　In the perusal of these volumes and handling
these valuable relics, we may be confident, much of
his time was passed — that precious portion which after
the ordinary duties of life and the business of the world
were discharged, he might more peculiarly call his
own.　Collectors are a self-pleasing race, and their
happiness is in their cabinets and libraries.　As other
men take delight in their horses, their model farm,
or other form of more or less liberal recreation, so he
rejoiceth with a black letter page open before him, in
the rarity of a coin, or a splendid impression of an
early engraving.　The taste is more engrossing than
that for many other hobbies, since it can be more
steadily gratified.　It is good for all weathers, and is,
in fact, never out of season.　If not necessarily a virtue
in itself, it is closely allied to one.　The amateur, we
are aware, does not always read the books or profit by
the treasures which he collects, but if he lose the benefit himself, he not unfrequently guards and preserves
what others may enjoy — and so entitles himself to the
credit of a helper to the race.　But it is not likely that
great collections are often made without profit to the
owner ; since the acquisition requires the cultivation
of taste, drscrimination and perseverance ; and, lavish
of expense in one direction, demands self-denial in
others.　Collectors are generally temperate and frugal,
and their employments, upon the whole, are of a rational cast.　Ridicule will, of course, be heaped upon

the fraternity. Men who ride hobbies must expect to
be laughed at by people whose hobbies are of a different color; yet, seeing what enemies to a man's
peace there are in the world, it is perhaps wise to che-
rish a self-pleasing delusion of some kind or other, and
well would it be for the world if this was always as
innocent as that which leads in the direction of literature and art. A plea may be put in even for the "Illustrator,"—a weakness of comparatively recent in-
vention. Everybody remembers the will of the virtuoso Nicholas Gimcrack in the Tatler, in which that
eccentric testator, much to their mortification, be-
queaths his extraordinary rarities to his kinsmen. But
among them all, his mummies, crocodile's eggs, and
last year's collection of grasshoppers, et cetera, there
is nothing which has anything to do with books and
engravings. The genius of "Illustration" had not
then dawned upon the world. Few of the strokes of
humor of the old satirists would have hit our friend
John Allan, unless perchance in a suspicious number
of snuff boxes which he possessed — a weakness, by
the way, which he shared with no less a personage
than Frederick the Great, and an alarming number of
old watches; but these were nothing to his leading
passion for "Illustration."

As for the snuff boxes, a person unacquainted with
the peculiar disposition of antiquarians, might suppose,
at the sight of a hundred of these articles, and the
goodly array of punch ladles alongside of them —
among which was one especially provocative of con-

viviality, if, as alleged, it once belonged to Robert
Burns; one might, we say, at the sight of these
things, readily imagine that the owner of all this in-
flammatory apparatus was an inveterate snufftaker, and
a jolly companion over his cups. Quite the contrary
was the case. Mr. Allan indulged, if this is a true
expression for such an affliction, in the use of tobacco
in no form; while, without any pretensions to absti-
nence, few men in the country could say that during
so long a life, including, too, the good old hard drinking
era, they had, in a slang phrase of our times, "pu-
nished" so little liquor. Looking at the habits of the
man, one might regard his passion for the acquisition
of snuff boxes in the light of a raid upon the enemy,
or a species of confiscation with a view to the public
good, or, perhaps, rather a desire to preserve a curious
memorial of a barbarism of the past, as thumb screws,
iron boots of the Inquisition, and slave shackles, are
treasured up in public museums. Yet a more agreeable view of the matter might be taken, contemplating
the snuff boxes as emblems of the graceful personal
attentions of gentlemen of the old school, opening the
way to many pleasant acquaintanceships; and the ladles not as dispensers of remorse in the potent material
fiery liquid of unseemly debaucheries, but of the intellectual aroma of the banquet, the kindling fancies,
the play of wit, the vivid heart utterances which Bac-
chus is supposed to engender.

The origin of the mania of "Illustration," is traced
to the publication of the Rev. James Granger's Biog-

raphical History of England, arranged for the insertion
of portraits in the latter **portion** of the last century.
The plan which he threw out was accepted ; a new
pleasure was invented for collectors, and they eagerly
availed themselves of it. Rare volumes of all sorts
were ransacked and plundered to furnish the coveted
portraits—a spoliation thus alluded to by Ireland in
his satiric poem, " Chalcographimania :"—

> Granger—whose biographic page,
>
> Hath prov'd for years so much the rage ;
>
> That scarce one book its portrait graces,
>
> Torn out, alas ! each author's face is.

And more wittily by the learned Dr. Ferriar, detector
of the plagiarisms of Sterne, in a poetical Epistle to
Richard Heber, the famed book collector : —

> " Now warn'd by Oxford and by Granger school'd,
>
> In paper-books, superbly gilt and tool'd,
>
> He pastes, from injur'd volumes snipt away,
>
> His *English Heads*, in chronicled array.
>
> Torn from their destin'd page, (unworthy meed
>
> Of knightly counsel and heroic deed),
>
> Not Faithorne's stroke, nor Field's own types can save
>
> The gallant Veres, and one-eyed Ogle brave.
>
> Indignant readers seek the image fled,
>
> And curse the busy fool, who *wants a head*."

Dibdin, in his " Bibliomania," has in a few words hit
off the passion with a saving clause for its rational indulgence. " If judiciously treated," says he, " illustrating is of all the symptoms the least liable to mis-
chief. To possess a series of well executed portraits

4

of illustrious men, at different periods of their lives,
from blooming boyhood to phlegmatic old age, is sufficiently amusing ; but to possess every portrait, *bad,
indifferent and unlike,* betrays such a dangerous and
alarming symptom as to render the case almost incur-
able.

There have been some other very clever satires on
the folly. The Rev. James Beresford, the author of
that amusing book, " The Miseries of Human Life,"
in an essay entitled " Bibliosophia," elicited by Dibdin's
publication just mentioned, thus pictures the Genius
of Illustration : " Here the type-fount and the copper
plate are beheld in a constant, though amicable contest.
Page and plate—page and plate—page and plate, keep
on together in wedded harmony (" concordia dis-
cors"), through a lengthening career of delight. * *
Let the historian but obliquely allude to a long-for-
gotten name,—and, with stupendous alacrity, the
POWER OF ILLUSTRATION has dragged the world of curiosity for every *effigy,* genuine or spurious, by every gra-
ver, of every age, from every country, in every degree
of excellence, and in every stage of preservation, down
to the last dregs of ruin :—*Io triumphe!*—*there* they are,
and *in* they shoal upon the groaning, bursting volume !
—Let the writer but have innocently hinted that his
hero or his hero's cousin, had a house to live in,—
and, while the press is working the intelligence, representation upon representation of the last rafter of
every dwelling, suspected to have been *once visited* by
either, is ready to push into its place !—Did an illus-

trious (and accordingly illustrated) personage, ever sit
down ?—*there* is his chair,—or, at least, a leg of it.
Did he ever write ?— *There* are his pot hooks and hang-
ers.—Did he like a late venerable Prelate, occasionally
relax from " the toils of study, by watching the drol-
leries of his kitten ?—There is Puss ?"

Mr. Allan was fond of these satires upon his favorite
amusement ; the passages we have cited being all taken
from valued books in his collection.   He would laugh
with the wits at the folly, shrug his shoulders at the
expense—and go on collecting, delighted to the end.
He cultivated one capital preservative against re-
proach ;—he paid on the instant, kept no bills, and never remembered the cost. Sometimes he had his doubts
and compunctions, and would tell his friend the im-
porter John Wiley, that " he had taken the pledge,"
and would order no more books from Europe ; but as
with most teetotalers his self-denying resolutions were
badly kept.   A tempting catalogue would again per-
suade him ; and new purchases kept coming in to the
last.   A rare copy of Wither's Poems was on its way
to him when he died.

The satires we have quoted exhibit the perversions of a
pursuit which, kept within its proper limits, has its com-
mendable uses.   It very readily runs into abuse, indeed,
and its fair opportunities are narrowly circumscribed.
But much good may be done by a judicious illustrator
who in his legitimate sphere may be regarded as a pic-
torial annotator.   Thus a correct and well engraved
portrait is always desirable, when the subject is of suf-

ficient importance in the text to excite a rational curiosity. The mere circumstance of a name being mentioned there is not enough ; it should be in some substantial connection with the book. If the subject of the page, for instance, be Dr. Johnson, in a volume of literary biographies, a good engraving from the portraits by Reynolds, or Opie, or Barry, will be welcome; but if the learned Doctor chance to indulge in a quotation from Horace or Lucretius, it is simply an impertinence, for no better reason, to intrude real or pretended representations of those classic worthies. Yet absurdities of this kind are often practised to the detriment of otherwise well prefaced volumes. Historical works and books of memoirs admit of liberal portrait illustration. It is an offence in a publisher to issue a biography without a portrait of the subject, where one can be obtained. If good pictures of the scenery amidst which he grew up and by which his character was influenced, can be added, these too are highly desirable. Only let them be like good notes, really valuable aids to the text, and they will hardly be superfluous, unless the book be overloaded with them. Beyond a certain number, it is better that they should be classified and arranged by themselves as collections of engravings. As for stripping good books of these plates to decorate others, it deserves the censure of the satirist ; but on the other hand, as an offset, the " illustrators" are entitled to the credit of rescuing many engravings from volumes and magazines destined to perish ; and they have stimulated publishers to issue

new plates for the express purpose of supplying the
wants of the collector. Upon the whole, literature has
probably gained more than it has lost by the mania.
American history, the chosen field of book illustration,
by our countrymen, has certainly profited. Thousands
of valuable engravings have been sought out and preserved from oblivion by transfer from their ragged
homes, in old decaying magazines and broken volumes, to the luxurious quarters of large paper editions,
where purified from the stains of time and extended by
Trent, they enjoy in their age a glory unknown to their
youth. The story of the American Revolution and the
memory of Washington in particular, already owe
much to the zeal of the illustrators, as the most in-
credulous may be convinced by glancing at such volumes as those of Sparks and Irving, in the possession
of Mr. John B. Moreau—prepared by him with nice
tact and discrimination, consummate nicety of workmanship, and every way by map, portrait, and other
engravings, a welcome aid to the historical enquirer, as
well as a pleasure in the perusal, to the man of taste.
What has been thus done for Washington, in this and
other instances, is being extended to the other fathers
of the state. The labors of the engraver are in demand for the purpose, and photography—as it ad-
vances as an art, is rapidly gaining ground with the
" illustrators," who have hitherto handled it rather
shyly, fearful of the durability of its pictures. Its ready
resources, in reproducing rare prints, and reducing and

copying old family pictures, cannot fail to be appreciated.

Mr. Allan's taste for the preservation of scrap books of engravings is said to have been developed at an early age, when he laid the fireside almanac under contribution; boys are apt thus to mutilate books, but he knew how to preserve them as well. The first impulse of a decided character which led him to book illustration, came with his correspondence with the eminent London print seller, Evans, some thirty years since. He wished to obtain some amusing sporting prints for the recreation of his children, and requested a friend in London to procure them. The order was placed in the hands of Colnaghi, who executed it on the most liberal scale, with a supply of hunting scenes from the Scottish Highlands to India—with a bill of proportional extent. This was beyond the purchaser's wants. He resold many of the plates in New York, and sent out a particular description of what he required. The new order was handed to Mr. Evans, and judiciously filled, and the correspondence resulted in opening a channel for the supply of prints for illustration, an object which Mr. Allan thenceforth pursued with avidity. Many of the best works of this class, which he came to possess, as a valuable copy of Burns' Poems, a folio of portraits of Mary Queen of Scots, with scenes illustrating her career, Ireland's Calcographimania, and others, were prepared for him by Evans, and afforded an excellent model for his own labors — for labors they were, though coupled with amusement, in which he found himself engaged. It would be curious to calculate the number of hours, many of them gained from sleep by his habit of early rising, spent by Mr. Allan in carefully extending octavo pages to quarto, and seeking for and inserting portraits and scenes alluded to in the text. Some hundred volumes, which found liberal purchasers at the sale, were thus literally manufactured by him. He was a pioneer in this country in the pursuit, the foremost in point of time of the American illustrators.

Among the most curious and entertaining of his illustrated books, perhaps the best generally known in his collection and the first enquired for by visitors, were the volumes of Knickerbocker's History of New York. For this veritable chronicle he had a particular regard. Its humor, broad fun and rollicking gayety, were quite to his taste; and he eagerly seized upon the work as an appropriate vehicle for the display of the numerous curious and valuable Dutch prints with which his scrap books and portfolios always abounded. With a stock of engravings from the paintings of Teniers, Ostade, and other hearty old artists, from whom, it may be supposed, the author himself had drawn no little of his humorous inspiration, it was not a difficult nor altogether an inappropriate task to "illustrate" the pages of the venerable Diedrich, which, to meet the emergency, were inlaid and extended from the modest duodecimo of the original edition to the liberal margin of a small folio or quarto. The feastings and revelry, the St. Nicholas festivities, and other quaint pictures of manners of the old Dutch masters, were indeed singularly in harmony with the work; while to facilitate the undertaking, a number of interesting engravings had been lately published in London to accompany the book, from the pencils of those admirable artists Leslie and Washington Allston, who were stimulated by friendship to lend their best powers to the undertaking. George Cruikshank also made it the subject of some of his earlier and best etchings. Beside these obvious and more appropriate illustrations, Mr. Allan, doubtless encouraged by the liberties taken by the author with the old New York families, with the zeal of a genuine " illustrator," did not hesitate to press any odd engraving into the service which might raise an additional laugh at the expense of the already over ridiculed Knickerbockers. These he occasionally inscribed with comments of his own, neatly underwritten ; for example, accompanying an excruciating picture of some barber's surgical operation in the agonies of which the Dutch school delighted, with this description : —"Dr. Onderdonk performing an operation over the left eye of Mynheer Van Der Spiegel, occasioned by an accident when catching shad off the Fort in company with Jacobus Van Tassel, Garret Van Bummell and Anthony Van Winkle."

Another of these engravings by Visscher, in one of the larger volumes picturing an untrussed burgher held down by three dames who are vigorously administering blows with palm and ferula, is inscribed, " The mode of punishing a drunken, unruly husband, practiced by the ladies of New Amsterdam in the days of Wouter Van **Twiller."**   A stout, one-legged hero, evidently a Chelsea pensioner, does duty **for** Peter Stuyvesant; an exaggerated figure of Punch, right leg extended, with his customary prominence of nose, **is** labelled, " Mynheer Beekman :" while, on looking over one of the volumes, we found a well known engraving of our portly old friend Dr. **Parr,** smoking his **pipe as** usual with his plethora of **self-conceit,** introduced as " **Mynheer Hardenbroeck** become wealthy and powerful."

It was an odd amusement, this fantastic effort of Mr. Allan, to ridicule the ridiculous ;——a broad joke, **of** course—the very riot of an " illustrator." He undoubtedly " slaughtered" a great many choice prints in the operation, for it was necessary to disguise them by cutting off titles and occasionally to meet the exigencies of the page, the names of artist and engraver, —a malpractice of which so earnest an appreciator of the art should not have been guilty ; but " illustrators," as we have intimated, do not stick at trifles.

In many of those books so comprehensively described by Charles Lamb as those which no " gentleman's library should be without"—the standard publications of the Trade,—Mr. Allan's library was, no doubt, deficient,—though it was not ill supplied with works of sound literature. Thus, for instance, we find Locke and Hume, the latter of whom Mr. Allan was too good a Scotchman to neglect, with a noticeable absence of Gibbon, of whose writings the catalogue of his library

does not furnish a single item. The English poets are,
in general, tolerably well represented, with a falling
off, at the end, in the omission of Wordsworth and
Tennyson. But ample amends for any neglect of this
kind was made in his collection of rare editions of the
old English poets of the seventeenth century. The
miscellaneous volumes of biography, memoirs, pictures
of manners, exhibit a good taste in reading. Works
relating to Scotland, and especially to Burns and Ayr-
shire, were, as might be expected, numerous. It is,
however, in the light of the special collection of a virtuoso and amateur of the fine arts, that the library is
to be regarded. For the ordinary standard books never
out of print, Mr. Allan could go to the Society Library,
of which he was a member; what he prided himself
upon was the possession of out of the way works rarely
to be met with. It was this which gave a peculiar
value to his collection, and invested his house with such
an interest, that admission to it was esteemed a privi-
lege by cultivated students. It was a rare treat to those
fortunate enough to possess his acquaintance to be received and introduced by him to the treasures of his
shelves, uniting the charms of literature and art, which
were freely laid open to his friends with genial alacrity.
It is the occasional failing or vice of collectors to be
selfish and unsocial and display a miserly jealousy in
the care of their possessions; but there was nothing of
this reserve or churlishness about Mr. Allan. He was
ever ready to exhibit his stores and allow others to
profit by them; he would willingly explain their value,

and permit notes to be made of his books, which is
certainly all that should be asked.   He would even, on
occasion, lend a volume; but this, as it was in general
contrary to good manners to insist upon, was opposed
to his settled principles to grant.   His private opinion
on this subject may be readily understood by the perusal of the following card, found among his papers,
which, for the benefit of all possessors of valuable
libraries, we here present in fac simile.

LENDING BOOKS

An Ancient Writer says, in reference to the custom of lending books, that, To lend a book is to lose it, and borrowing but a hypocritical pretence for Stealing.

The neat and somewhat formal penmanship of this
card will not fail to be remarked.   It is an accomplish-
ment seldom cultivated in these days to any great extent,
but one in acquiring which Mr. Allan had taken much
pains.   In the index to the catalogue of his library, Mr.
Sabin refers to twenty-seven works bearing more or
less directly on penmanship, among them numerous
copy books with round text and various flourishes of
the old masters of the art.

In matters relating to the Fine Arts, Mr. Allan's collection was catholic and comprehensive, embracing specimens of the great engravers of the old German, Dutch, French, Italian and English schools. For the ancient school of Albert Durer, and his followers, he had a liking, which, taken in connection with his fondness for the old Emblem designers, showed an advanced taste in the appreciation of the profounder elements of art. He appeared interested in every form of decoration proceeding from the burin, from the simply pretty and agreeable of Cipriani redeemed from insipidity by the workmanship of Bartolozzi, through the sensuous French school of Picart, to the devotional themes and lofty serenity of the great Masters. His library contained rare materials for the study of the art of engraving, and here his passion for illustration appeared peculiarly appropriate.

There were doubtless many interesting incidents relating to the purchase of the curious books which made up Mr. Allan's collection. These old volumes, treasured by their owners from generation to generation, might disclose much that would be worthy of reflection, could they tell of their various fortunes, as they passed from library to library, till the vicissitudes of men and families opened a way for them across the Atlantic. On some of them the record was written in the autographs of former distinguished persons. One we noticed bore the signature of Dean Swift. Numerous peculiarities are mentioned in the catalogue.

Then there were the lucky chances in obtaining the eagerly sought for treasure.

The story of the purchase of one of the rarest volumes of the collection is, perhaps, worth preserving. A genuine Scotchman, addicted of course to devotion to the memory of Burns, Mr. Allan had long desired to become the possessor of the Kilmarnock, the first edition of the poet's writings. Though seldom to be met with, a copy occasionally turned up in Scotland, and an order was sent to a well known bookseller of Edinburgh, to pay as much as five guineas for one, which was considered a good price. The bookseller wrote in reply, that he had a copy at eight guineas; Mr. Allan rose to this, but before his order reached the dealer the book was sold. It happened after this, that a friend of Mr. Allan, from Scotland, an architect and bridge builder, visited him in his house in New York, and, on taking his leave, asked " if he could do any thing for him at home." " Get me, if you can, the Kilmarnock edition of Burns," was Mr. Allan's reply, and his friend was duly instructed as to its scarcity and value, and the price he might have to pay. On his return, he was engaged, as usual, in his engineering occupations in the country, when one of his workmen, too fond of " Scotch drink," came to him desiring to receive his wages for a broken week to celebrate a holiday. Knowing the propensities of the man the money was withheld with the expectation of retaining him at his work; but the next day, and for several days after, the man was missing. On making his ap-

pearance again, he was questioned as to his absence;
" he had been off," he said, ".some distance." " But
how could you go without the money?" " I raised it
by pledging some books at the pawnbroker's on which
I received ten shillings." " What books had *you?*" he
was asked, with some incredulity. " Oh! a copy of
Burns, among others. Every Scotchman, you know,
has Burns." " What sort of a copy was it?"—recollection of his friend across the Atlantic beginning to
glimmer in the mind of the inquirer. " The old Kilmarnock edition," was the reply, and the recollection
was established. " Now," said the employer, adroitly
managing the subject so as not to excite expectation or
alarm, " suppose I should relieve you of this business,
what do you want for your pawnbroker's ticket?" " I
will take a guinea." After some haggling as to who
should in that case pay the pawnbroker his ten shillings, which resulted, we believe, in splitting the dif-
ference, the money was paid and the book secured.
Thus the long coveted prize came to the hands of Mr.
Allan, in America, and cost its possessor nothing but
the gratitude, which, to be sure, is something ecstatic,
of a delighted bibliomaniac.

It was not often that Mr. Allan made marginal or
other written comments in his books; but in one instance, at least, he appears to have taken particular
pains to record his impressions. His regard for Burns
called forth this expression of feeling. For the good
fame of this national author he was a stickler, repu-
diating utterly the harsh censoriousness of those who

would obscure the virtues of a man of genius by
studiously setting forth his occasional aberrations. He
believed with Wordsworth, who published a manly
expostulation on this theme,* that there was something
better to be thought of over the grave of Burns, than
the loves and revels of which he had repented. In the
goodly row of illustrated volumes of Burns, which occupied his shelves, there was one which provoked Mr.
Allan's scorn. It was a homily and a very ill judged
one, full of spite and temper, on the text of Burns's
failings, published after his death, arraigning his ad-
mirers for their devotion to his memory, and denoun-
cing him as an " irreligious profligate," " a profane
blackguard," with sundry similar comments on what
the writer is pleased to call his profanity, cruelty,
intemperance and so forth. Among other remarks,
it is chronicled of the poet, " he was an enthusiastic
admirer of Wallace. He used to travel six miles on
Sunday to visit and examine the retreats and fastnesses
of his hero." The title of this absurd volume, published in Edinburgh in 1811, is " Burnomania: the
Celebrity of Robert Burns considered, in a discourse
addressed to real Christians of every denomination."
Mr. Allan's remarks, written in front of the book, are
as follows : " This work has been written by some
intolerant, religious, bigoted fanatic, one of the ' unco

* A Letter to a friend of Robert Burns : occasioned by an
intended republication of the account of the life of Burns, by
Dr. Currie ; and of the selection made by him from his letters.
By William Wordsworth. London, 1816. 8vo. pp. 37.

gude and rigidly righteous,' one who would consign
to Hell all but his own narrow sect. He is a coward
to attack the dead who can make no reply, ' But the
meanest rogue may burn a city, or kill a hero, whereas
he could neither build the one nor equal the other.'
Burns was fifty years in advance of the age in which
he lived ; had he lived when the writer of this pens
these lines, he would have been hailed as one inspired.
1842. But the cowardly assassin's shot falls harmless.
Burns's fame lives, and will continue to increase with
increasing splendour, and will survive the whole host
of religious knaves and hypocrites who have tried to
blast his fame.

> " Priests' hearts rotten, black as muck,
> " Lay stinking vile in every neuk !

" Omitted in most editions.—*Tam O'Shanter.*"

On the opposite page, Mr. Allan has added, " What
would he say of Byron, Moore, and a host of others,
who have sprung up since Burns. This work, I have
ascertained since, was written by a Reverend Dr. Peebles, of Ayr—1843. Has he not gone down

> " ' To the vile dust from whence he sprung
> Unwept, unhonored and unsung.'
>
> " ' Priests of all religions are the same.'

" The odium theologicum, or theological hatred, is pro-
verbial—revenge reigns with the greatest force in
Priests. This fellow *Peebles* would have sent *Burns* to
the dungeon and stake, if he had the power."

Mr. Allan, as we have intimated, gave directions
that his library and collections should be sold after his

death. In furtherance of this purpose, during the last month of his life, he.had been engaged with Mr. Sabin in the preparation of a catalogue of his books, which he lived to see nearly completed. It was placed in the printers' hands in January, with the addition of a careful list of the Engravings arranged by Mr. Dexter, the accomplished print dealer of Broadway—a tribute of regard to the memory of his old acquaintance. Voluntary assistance of this kind was also rendered by others of Mr. Allan's friends. When the catalogue was sufficiently forwarded, the sale was announced by Messrs. Bangs, Merwin & Co., to commence on the 2d of May, 1864. The books were removed to their auction rooms on Broadway, and were on exhibition for a fortnight, during which they attracted a large number of intelligent inquirers, prominent among whom—a new feature in exhibitions of this class—were many ladies, who carefully inspected the works on the fine arts. When the sale commenced on the appointed day Mr. Merwin the auctioneer announced his intention to get through the catalogue of the books numbering over three thousand lots the first week, which required him to sell an average of about five hundred lots each day, or about an hundred lots an hour, the time occupied being between four in the afternoon and half past nine in the evening. This was accomplished without break or hesitation, unless we except a few minutes interruption one day when an evening newspaper was brought into the room and a passage read aloud by one of the company giving an

6

account of a preliminary movement of Gen. Grant's campaign across the Rapidan, and on another similar occasion the sale was suspended while a city regiment, which had its drill room above stairs was leaving for special duty in the harbor. Eager competition was manifested for the books from the beginning, the average of prices far outrunning any previous instance of the kind in the country. This was due to the specialty of the collection and the increased demand among wealthy purchasers for rarities of the class offered. The following statement of each of the eleven days sale of the entire collection will show how well the demand was sustained in every department :

1st day, Lots	1— 557	books,	-	$3,789 39
2d " "	558—1,110	do.	-	4,874 84
3d " "	1,111—1,673	do.	-	6,083 43
4th " "	1,674—2,237	do.	-	3,905 41
5th " "	2,238—2,805	do.	-	4,072 75
6th " "	2,806—3,321	do.	-	4,333 14
7th " "	3,222—3,737	Autographs and Engravings,	- -	3,719 61
8th day, lots	3,7384—212	Engravings and Drawings,	- -	2,225 35
9th day, lots	4,2134—599	Coins, Medals and Minerals,	- -	1,140 39
10th day, lots	4,600—4,951	Minerals and Snuff Boxes,	- -	870 13
11th day, lots	4,952—5,278	Watches, China, &c.,	- -	2,674 82

Exhibiting a total of $37,689.26, assuredly a liberal

amount when compared with the prudent estimate of
Mr. Allan, who spoke of the probable auction returns
of the whole at about twelve thousand dollars. The
sale was not only well sustained throughout, but many
of the prices paid were extraordinary ; nineteen volumes produced over a hundred dollars each, and two
items were run up to over a thousand. The highest
priced book was the best illustrated of the Knickerbocker volumes, of which we have spoken, which was
knocked down to the agent, Mr. French, at twelve
hundred and fifty dollars. Next to this was the mis-
sionary Eliot's translation of the Bible into the Indian
language, which was bought by Mr. Bouton, the bookseller, for eight hundred and twenty-five dollars, an
enormous increase in the sum paid for a copy at the
sale of Mr. Corwin's books, in 1856. It then brought
two hundred and ten dollars, a price which was much
talked of in those days. A copy of Walton and Cotton's
Angler, the two volumes of Pickering's edition, extended to four and richly illustrated, brought six hundred dollars. A valuable copy of Dibdin's Bibliomania,
in two volumes, 900 on the catalogue, extended and
choicely illustrated with portraits, formerly in the possession of Mr. Town, and noticed by Dibdin himself in
one of his books, brought three hundred and sixty
dollars a volume. The folio volume of the engraved
portraits of Mary Queen of Scots produced three hundred and seventy-five dollars. A finely illustrated
Burns, in 5 vols. 8vo, No. 462 on the catalogue, forty
dollars a volume. The Kilmarnock Burns, the story

of the acquisition of which we have related, one hundred and six dollars. A valuable inlaid illustrated copy of Byron's English Bards and Scotch Reviewers, with portraits and autographs, was bought by Mr. Farnum, of Providence, R. I., for one hundred and thirty dollars. Fifty-six volumes were sold for fifty dollars and over.

In the miscellaneous department of the sale, there was the same generous competition. A fragment of a letter written by Robert Burns, lot No. 3,337, brought forty-five dollars ; Benjamin Franklin's post office account, a very neat manuscript, twenty dollars ; while an autograph of Gen. Washington, a letter in reply to the address of the corporation of New York conferring upon him the freedom of the city, in 1785, was knocked down at the extraordinary sum of two thousand and fifty dollars. This unprecedented bid was explained by the circumstance of two agents competing with one another, without limitation from their principals. That famous relic, the Burns' toddy-ladle, lot 5,053, was bought at one hundred and ten dollars, for Mr. J. V. L. Pruyn, of Albany.

So closed the sale of Mr. Allan's collections. Many of the books, engravings and other rarities which he valued, fell into the hands of his friends, who will think more highly of them in remembrance of the kind and cheerful gentleman by whom they were so long preserved.

E. A. D.

20 Clinton Place, New York,
　　May, 1864.

MR. ALLAN'S BOOK PLATE.